A Date with Dad
Text Copyright ©2020 by LaToyia Jones

Illustrations by Jay Wallace
Edited by Eryka Parker of Lyrical Innovations, LLC

Book cover photo copyright © 2020 by LaToyia Jones
ISBN 978-1-7359671-0-3
First Edition

DEDICATION

To all the little girls who gaze at the open sky at night and see an opportunity to create engaging new worlds in their minds. Let Poa be your guide as you explore the countless possibilities this life can bring.

THE ADVENTURES OF POA PRESENTS

A Date with Dad

Written by Latoyia Jones

Illustrated by Josh G. Wallace

Hi, friend! I'm Poa, which is pronounced "POH-AH". I'm 5 years old.

Want to know a cool secret?

I have a really BIG imagination and I become a superhero at night!

Guess what else!

I'm going on a date with my dad tomorrow.

See? He left me
a note. He wrote
it himself.

But wait, what is a date?

Do you know what a date is, friend?

I think I'll go ask my mom.

7

Mom!!

What is a date?

Poa, what's got you so excited?

9

Look, Mom! Dad is taking me on a date!
But I do not know what that is.

Do you know what a date is?

Sure, I do. It's when you and someone special do something fun together. It looks like Dad has an amazing adventure planned, just for the two of you!

Oh, I can't wait. Tomorrow, I'm going on an adventure with my dad!

Yes, but tonight you are going to bed.

Sweet dreams, Poa.
Tomorrow will be a
big day. Good night.

I'm going on an adventure
with my Dad tomorrow.

I'm going on an adventure
with my Dad tomorrow.

I'm going on an adventure with my Dad tomorrow.

Now, I close my eyes to sleep.
I wonder who in my dreams I'll meet.
As my imagination runs free,
I wonder just who Poa will be.

Well, this is it, Poa. Our special date. Do you know where we are?

Whoa, Dad! This place is awesome. It's not a zoo, is it?

No, but you are close. For our date,
I wanted to take you on a wild adventure.

We are on a safari.

What is a safari?

A safari is a trip to see animals, but it takes place in their natural home. In a zoo, a home is created for the animals. Look at that animal over there, Poa!

Oh! That one has a really long neck and lots of spots. And look, it's eating leaves off that tree.

Hey friend, do you know what animal this is?

I bet you guessed it's a giraffe and that answer is right.

Friend, did you know that a group of giraffes is called a tower and that they are the tallest animals in the world?

Wow! Dad, where are we?

We are on the moon, Poa. For our special date, I wanted to take you on an adventure that was out of this world.

This is the moon? Why are there so many holes? I thought the moon was round and smooth.

The moon is a big rock. When small rocks crash into the moon, they leave holes behind.

How did you do that, Dad?

Poa, there's less gravity here.

Gravity?
What is gravity?

Gravity is a force that pulls people and things down to the ground.

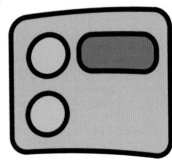

Oh.
But I can't see it.

*No one can see it, Poa.
It's invisible and, on the
moon, the force of gravity
is less than it is on earth.
That's why I can jump so
high, and you can too.*

Oh, can we play a game to see who can jump higher?

We sure can. Think you can beat me?

It looks like Poa is enjoying her dream about exploring the moon with her Dad!
What do you think is next?

For our special date,
I wanted to take you on
a quest to tickle your
taste buds!

There are ice cream floats,
ice cream sundaes, and
ice cream sandwiches.

31

Dad, this is incredible! I've never seen so many flavors of ice cream in all my adventures!

All this ice cream looks so yummy and there are so many flavors to choose from.

There are also lots of colors, like pink, blue, and green ice cream, too!

Yes, and there is ice cream with fruit, ice cream with nuts, and even ice cream with sprinkles.

I think I'd like to try pink bubblegum, vanilla bean, and blueberry dream!

Great choices, Poa. And you know what else?

What else, Dad?

After our adventure here, you, mom, and I are going to make our own ice cream at home.

Hooray! Wait... I've never made ice cream before. I can't wait! **Would you like to make your own ice cream too, friend? What flavors do you like?**

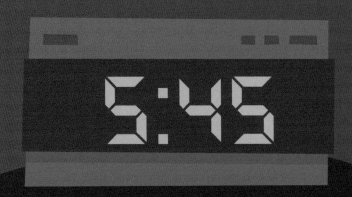

I know where we are now, Dad. •
We have been here before. We're in a movie theater.

Yes, but not just any movie theater, Poa.
For our date, I wanted to take you on an epic
adventure. Here, put these on.

This is a 3D movie, Poa. In most movies, things and people on the screen are flat, like the pictures we draw on paper.

But in a 3D movie, things and people seem to be right in front of us. Or all around us.

That's right, Poa, and that's because they are made with two cameras, and because of these special glasses, which allow us to see in 3D.

Well, get ready for some action coming right atcha!

I'm ready! **What about you, friend?**
Are you ready for some 3D action?

Good morning, friend!
Did you see all of my amazing dreams?
Today's the big day.
I can't wait for my date tonight!

Are we going on safari?

Safari? No, Poa, but we are going to have a wild time.

Are we going to the moon?

We won't go that far, Poa, but I promise our adventure will be out of this world.

What about ice cream? Are we going to get ice cream?

No, but tonight is going to be a real treat for both of us.

How about the movies?
Are we going to see a 3D movie?

No, but this adventure
will be like nothing
you have ever seen.

Oh, Dad,
what is it?
Those were
are all the
places I visited
in my dreams.

44

Oh, Poa, I can promise you it will be just as magical as any dream you have ever had. Come on, get dressed. Let's get Mom so she can help you get ready.

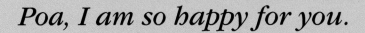

Poa, I am so happy for you.

I can't wait, Mom!

I know that you are in for an awesome adventure... There. All set, Poa. You look beautiful.

46

Wow, Poa. What a great choice for our date tonight!
Okay, let's get going. Our adventure awaits!

Oh, wow, Dad.
A big dance!
It's all my friends, and their dads too!

Isn't it wonderful, Poa?

Yes, it is! And this is what
I dreamed about.

It is? But we are not on the moon, we are not on safari, we are not at the ice cream shop, and we are not at the movies.

I know, but Dad, it is just as magical, just like you said! I dreamed of the moon, and when we left home, I looked up and saw the brightest moon I have ever seen.

I dreamed of seeing animals on a safari and look over there! That dad is making balloon animals for every little girl. I see a giraffe, a monkey, and an elephant, too.

I dreamed of all kinds of ice cream flavors and right next to the table with cake and punch, a dad is giving out big scoops.

I dreamed we went to the movies and there is a big screen right over there with pictures in 3D. Dad, all of my dreams came true. Thank you for an amazing adventure!

You are welcome, Poa.
There will be many
more like this one.
Just wait and see.
Now, let's dance!